RAINFORESTS

RAINFORESTS

PETER MURRAY

THE CHILD'S WORLD®, INC.

PHOTO CREDITS

Comstock: cover, 2, 6, 9, 10, 13, 16, 20, 23, 24, 26, 29
Dembinsky Photo Associates/Ira Rubin: 23
Dembinsky Photo Associates/Doug Locke: 15, 19, 30

Printed in the United States of America.

Library of Congress Cataloging-in-Publication Data
Murray, Peter, 1952 Sept. 29-
Rainforests / Peter Murray
p.   cm.
Includes index.
Summary: Briefly describes rainforests, telling where
they are found and what lives there, particularly in
the upper levels known as the canopy.
ISBN 1-56766-278-1   (lib. bdg.)
1. Rain forest ecology—Juvenile literature.
2. Forest canopy ecology—Juvenile literature.
3. Rain forests—Juvenile literature.
[1. Rain forests.]   I. Title.
QH541.5.R27M88   1996
574.5'2642—dc20   96-10951
                               CIP
                               AC

TABLE OF CONTENTS

Welcome to the Rainforest! 7

What Does the Rainforest Look Like? .11

How Does the Rainforest Grow? 14

What is the Rainforest Canopy? 17

What Plants Live in the Rainforest? .21

What Animals Live in the Canopy? 22

Does it Rain in the Rainforest? 25

Where Are Rainforests Found? 27

Are Rainforests in Danger? 28

Why Are Rainforests Important? 31

Index & Glossary 32

From an airplane, the Amazon Rainforest looks like an endless sea of green. It stretches as far as you can see. The treetops are so thick and close together you can't see the ground. It looks as if you could jump out of the plane and the trees would catch you in their soft, leafy branches.

The trees of the Amazon Rainforest seem to stretch on forever

Another way to see the rainforest is to float down the Amazon River. The river is wide and slow. The rainforest comes right up to the edge of the water, a wall of branches and leaves and strange noises. Tall trees lean out over you. The banks are a tangle of roots and tall grasses and leafy bushes. You hear the screeching of parrots and the chatter of monkeys. A floating log blinks yellow eyes. It's not a log, it's an alligator!

From the water, the rainforest looks like a wall of branches and leaves

WHAT DOES THE RAINFOREST LOOK LIKE?

From the river's edge, the forest looks like a solid mass of plants. You need to cut through the twisted vines and dense brush to move deeper into the forest. Once you get away from the riverbank and into the rainforest, walking becomes easier. The inside of the rainforest is damp and shady. High above your head, thick layers of leaves screen the bright sunlight. Because the sunlight is blocked by all the trees, there are only a few plants growing near the ground. The forest floor is covered with dead leaves and twigs.

Inside the rainforest, thick layers of leaves screen the bright sunlight

You are surrounded by tall, brown tree trunks. Thick vines called **lianas** wrap around the trees, climbing toward the sunlight. Many of the larger trees have wide supports called **buttresses** at the base. The rainforest has only a thin layer of soil. Instead of reaching deep into the earth, the roots of rainforest trees spread out. The buttresses prop the trees up and keep them from falling over.

Buttresses keep the trees from falling over

HOW DOES THE RAINFOREST GROW?

Life comes and goes quickly in the rainforest. When a plant or an animal dies, it is quickly absorbed back into the **ecosystem**. Dead things do not last long on the warm, damp forest floor. Leaves and twigs are quickly broken down by termites, earthworms, fungi, and bacteria. As the dead plant matter **decomposes**, it **fertilizes** the surrounding plants. It provides **nutrients** to help the rainforest grow. Rainforest soil is not very fertile. This is because the tremendous number of plants growing in the forest use up nutrients almost as soon as they reach the soil.

Ants break down dead leaves on the rainforest floor

Millions of plant and animal **species** live in the rain-forest, but most of them never touch the ground. They live high in the trees, in the layer of leaves and branches called the **forest canopy**. In the rainforest, the canopy is where the action is. The canopy begins about 100 feet off the ground. It is hard for scientists to study the rainforest canopy because it is hard to reach. It would be much easier if you were a monkey!

The rainforest canopy is hard to reach

The rainforest canopy is made up of the leafy tops of hundreds of tree species. Many of them have familiar names. Teak and mahogany trees are used for making furniture. Rubber trees produce sap from which rubber is made. The Brazil nut tree provides us with big, tasty Brazil nuts. There are so many different kinds of trees in the forest that it is hard to find two that are the same. Some of them have only scientific names. And there are probably some kinds of trees yet to be discovered!

There are hundreds of tree species in the rainforest

WHAT PLANTS LIVE IN THE RAINFOREST?

Trees are not the only plants in the rainforest canopy. If you could travel through the canopy, leaping from tree to tree like a monkey, you would find thousands of smaller plants living high in the treetops, growing on the trees for support. This type of plant is called an **epiphyte**. Epiphytes do not damage the trees. They just grow on the trees to get closer to the sunlight.

Some of the most beautiful epiphytes are orchids. Orchids cling to trees with their roots, soaking up rainwater as it runs down the trunk.

An epiphytic orchid lives in the rainforest

WHAT ANIMALS LIVE IN THE CANOPY?

Most rainforest birds and animals live in the canopy. A single large tree can be home to many hundreds of species of animals. You might see a spider monkey, a slow-moving sloth, a long green boa constrictor, a family of brightly-colored parrots, and a bird-eating tarantula . . . and that would just be a start! If you looked closer, you might find a chameleon and six different species of tree frogs. And once you start counting the insects, look out! One scientist counted forty-three different species of ants on one rainforest tree!

A brightly colored parrot lives in the rainforest canopy

DOES IT RAIN IN THE RAINFOREST?

One thing you find plenty of in a rainforest is rain! The Amazon Rainforest gets about one hundred inches of rain each year. Sometimes it rains so long and so hard that the rivers rise over their banks and spill into the forests. The flooded forest is called the **varzea**. Fish swim in a world of underwater tree trunks. In the varzea, you might hear the gasping sigh of a pink dolphin, or see a flashing school of hungry piranhas. Fishermen pole through the varzea in their flat-bottomed canoes searching for tambaqui, a favorite food fish.

The rainforest floods when it rains

Central Africa, India, and Southeast Asia also have tropical rainforests. The plants and animals vary, but the ecosystem is similar. All the rainforests have a thick canopy of trees, thin soil, and a huge number of plant and animal species. If you were walking through the rainforest in Thailand, you might think you were in the Amazon—unless you ran into an orangutan or a tiger!

Orangutans live in tropical rainforests

ARE RAINFORESTS IN DANGER?

Today, the rainforests are being destroyed. Huge areas of rainforest are burned to the ground every day. The people who live near the rainforest need the land to grow food. When the forest is burned, the ashes combine with the thin soil to make good farmland—for a while. Unfortunately, after a few years, the soil is no longer any good. All its nutrients are used up. The thin soil blows away and the land goes to waste.

Rainforests are destroyed by people

Scientists believe that the rainforests must be saved if we want to keep living on this planet. The rainforests only cover six percent of the earth, but they are home to three-fourths of all our plant and animal species. Rainforests absorb **carbon dioxide** and give off **oxygen** through plant leaves, like giant air cleaners. They are called "the lungs of the world."

If the rainforests are destroyed, they cannot be replaced. It is up to all of us to save them.

GLOSSARY

buttresses (BUT-tress-is)
The broadened base of a tree trunk. Many rainforest trees have buttresses at the base.

carbon dioxide (CAR-bin die-OX-ide)
Heavy, colorless gas formed in animal respiration and in decay of plants and animals. Rainforest plants absorb carbon dioxide.

decomposes (dee-come-POSE-is)
To cause to rot. A leaf decomposes on the rainforest floor.

ecosystem (E-coe-sis-tem)
Animals and their environment functioning together. Rainforests are an important part of the Earth's ecosystem.

epiphyte (EPP-i-fite)
A plant that lives on a tree, using the tree for support. The rainforest has many epiphytes.

fertilizes (FUR-till-eye-zurs)
Any of a large number of materials spread on or worked into soil to increase its capacity to support plant growth. Dead plants and animals are fertilizers for the rainforest soil

forest canopy (FOR-est CAN-uh-pee)
A layer of leaves and branches high above the rainforest floor. Many different kinds of animals live in the rainforest canopy

lianas (Le-A-na)
Woody vines of tropical rainforests that root in the ground. Lianas wrap around rainforest trees.

nutrients (NEW-tree-ents)
Substances that provide life and growth. Rainforest soil is full of nutrients.

oxygen (OX-i-gin)
A colorless, tasteless, orderless gas. Plants give off oxygen through their leaves.

species (SPEE-sheez)
A group of plants or animals with similar characteristics. Hundreds of plant species live in the rainforest.

varzea (var-ZEE-a)
Pools formed when very heavy rains make rivers spill over their banks and flood the rainforest. Fish swim in the varzea.

INDEX

Amazon rainforest, 25

Amazon River, 8

animals 17, 22

destruction, 28, 31

epiphytes, 21

forest canopy, 17-18, 21-22

plants, 11, 12, 14, 17, 21

rain, 25

soil, 14, 28

species, 17, 18, 27

trees, 12, 18

varzea, 25